Simon the cross-bearer

A family is affected by their father's chance meeting with the Savior

by
Harry James Cargas

Publishing House
St. Louis

Copyright © 1979 by Concordia Publishing House
3558 South Jefferson Avenue, St. Louis, MO 63118

Library of Congress Catalog Card Number
ISBN 0-570-07977-2
Printed in the United States of America

Library of Congress Cataloging in Publication Data

Cargas, Harry J
    Simon the crossbearer.

    (Starlight books)
    SUMMARY: Simon the Cyrenean who was forced to carry the cross of Christ begins to see his role as one of honor, not shame.
    1. Simon of Cyrene—Juvenile fiction. [1. Simon of Cyrene—Fiction]
I. Title.
PZ7.C2144Si   [Fic]   78-12731
ISBN 0-570-07977-2

To SARITA JO CARGAS
whose joy and love
energize our family

Letter to the Reader

The writers of the four gospels (Matthew, Mark, Luke, and John) were given divine guidance in recording the birth of Jesus, His ministry, crucifixion, resurrection, and ascension. From the four Gospels we have learned that Jesus cured the sick, the lame, and the blind. He taught us how to live, how to pray, and how to treat others.

But Jesus touched many lives while here on earth for which there are no accounts. As Jesus and His followers walked from city to city, He no doubt met and talked with many people we know nothing about. But that is not important. What is important is that He lived and died for them and for us.

Jesus preached to 5,000 people at one time and fed them with five loaves and two fishes. Many people have wondered down through the years, "Whose lunch was it?" "How did he feel; what did he think?" The Bible doesn't tell us that, because that was not the important thing. What is important is that Jesus was able to feed 5,000 people with just two small fish and five loaves of bread.

But still we wonder: What would it have been like to have been there? to have seen, maybe even touched, Him? We can only guess. And, some people write stories about some of the people who might have come in contact with Jesus.

Simon the Crossbearer is such a fictional story. Simon, the Cyrenian, is mentioned by name in three of the four gospels, and in one reference his sons, Alexander and Rufus, are named. According to the accounts, Simon was "forced" to carry Jesus' cross.

What impact this incident might have had on his life and that of his family is not really known. We can only imagine. In our story, Simon, his family, and his friends accept Jesus as the Savior. That is the single important message in this book, and it is our sincere wish for you.

The Editor

Chapter 1

Passover time was approaching. The Jewish people celebrated the occasion one week out of every year in remembrance of the time when the head of each Hebrew household marked their doorposts with the blood of a lamb. This sign was used as a message for an angel, a minister of death. Wherever this angel saw the blood, he was not to enter; he was to "pass over" those houses. He was to bring grief only to the Pharaoh's people.

When he thought about it, Rufus felt a shiver run down his spine. He would have loved to have seen the angel. "Maybe I could have helped the angel," young Rufus often said to his mother. "I would have known which were the houses of the Hebrews," he mused. "I could have clued him in."

"That would have been very good," the boy's mother responded, smiling at the thought that God's angel would need help.

But that wasn't really what Passover time meant to him. It was a time of travel, of going to Jerusalem, and of playing with his cousin Matthew, and with Matthew's friends. Uncle Jacob's house was a great place, and Rufus looked forward to laughing and romping with those he loved but only got to see at special times.

The trip itself was long and tiring. Donkey riding was boring; the weather was hot; the route was dusty. Although Rufus and his brother Alexander complained, the traveling itself was always an adventure. Two years ago, while making the journey, the family was almost robbed by a band of thieves. The boys were terrified that the men might hurt their father. They knew that Simon was a strong man and had there been one or two bandits, or maybe even three, Simon could have adequately defended himself. But the odds were impossible. Luckily, a group of Roman soldiers were passing by at that moment and the robbers fled.

From that time on, Simon's family traveled with a group. It was safer.

On another one of their Passover trips to Uncle Jacob's house, Rufus' mother had helped to deliver a baby. As they walked along leading their donkey, a girl appeared from behind a cluster of boulders. She was out of breath and very anxious, pleading, "Oh please, friends, my mother is in need."

"What is the matter, child," Simon had responded in his typically kind way.

"Her baby is due," she said desperately, "and I don't know what to do."

Immediately, Rufus' mother took charge. "Is there anyone else in your family to aid you?" she inquired, already gathering things she would need to help. The girl told them that her father had died a few months ago, and that circumstances were such that she and her mother were traveling a short distance to be with a relative. The baby, however, was determined to be born sooner than was expected.

Rufus and his brother Alexander became very excited when they saw their mother direct their donkey towards the hidden place. She told the men of the family to wait. However, Simon insisted on going to have a look behind the rocks, first, to make certain that the girl was telling the truth. He had heard of the different tricks used by robbers to catch travelers off guard and he wasn't going to fall for anything like that.

When Simon saw the girl's mother in labor he quickly averted his eyes and returned, somewhat ashamed of his mistrust. "It is the times," he grumbled. His wife took over after that, and as he and Rufus and Alexander waited, tensely, a new life was welcomed—a wailing daughter whose strong cry indicated a truly healthy baby. The mother named the baby Ruth, after Rufus' mother. The family resumed the trip, and Simon insisted that their new friends continue the trip with them. Simon's wife could be heard humming hymns of thanksgiving to God for having been allowed to be a part of the great mystery of birth. Nothing could mar the joy for the rest of their trip.

"Are we going to visit little Ruth?" asked Rufus.

"We most certainly will," answered his mother. "She is three years old now."

On this current journey to Uncle Jacob's house, however, nothing in particular had happened. It was the kind of trip the parents hoped for, but which the boys had wished would have been more eventful.

But just outside the walls of Jerusalem the family found their progress stopped. They were at the back of a large, ever increasing crowd.

"What is the trouble?" Simon asked a fellow traveler.

"I have no idea," he responded wearily. "I am tired; I am thirsty, and I want only to get to the house of my brother and be rid of this dusty road."

Simon nodded in agreement. But, suddenly, the crowd began to cheer and shout. "Hosanna," they sang. Palm branches were being strewn about.

Slowly the crowd inched forward. The shouts of hosanna grew louder and louder.

"At least we're moving," Simon sighed.

He stretched himself to the full extent of his height. "It looks like a man riding a donkey," he reported.

"Is it a king like they're saying?" Alexander asked.

"Maybe Caesar!" Rufus added.

"No, I don't think so," answered Simon, cupping his hands over his eyes to get a clearer view. It appears to be... yes . . . just an ordinary man, not a Roman at all. He's riding . . . let's see . . . on a common *donkey*!" Simon's voice was tinged with disgust. The idea that he and his family and many other tired travelers should be so inconvenienced by a procession of people giving praise to a man on a donkey just plain angered him.

"Ouch," yelled Rufus. Someone had stepped on his toe. Ruth had dismounted the donkey and was walking alongside her husband. She reached out and in a motherly way took hold of her two sons' hands. Everyone settled

down and slowly inched their way toward Jerusalem with shouts of "Hosanna" filling the air.

* * *

"And, how was your journey?" Jacob asked, escorting his tired and weary relatives into his house. "No problems I hope?"

"No," answered Simon, already relieved that he had safely brought his family to the end of the first half of their journey. He would not totally relax until they were all back home in Cyrene. "We ran into a little problem just outside the gates of Jerusalem," he continued, brushing the dust from his clothing.

"We would have been here an hour ago, but we were held up by the strangest procession."

"Oh?" said Jacob with sincere concern. "What was the nature of the procession? Oh, don't tell me, I can guess. The Romans displaying their strength . . ."

"No," interrupted Rufus. "It was some man riding a donkey and lots and lots of people shouting . . . praises to . . ." Rufus' voice trailed off, when he realized that five pairs of eyes were trained on him. While he ordinarily would have liked the attention, he didn't like the look in his father's eyes.

After an awkward moment, Jacob cleared his throat and directed his next question to Simon. "Do you know who the man was? A Roman perhaps?"

"Ha!" laughed Matthew. "A Roman on a donkey. That's a joke!" It was Jacob's turn to cast his son a scolding look. Matthew lowered his eyes. Again there was a moment of silence, then Simon laughed. Ruth laughed too and it became infectious. Soon everyone was laughing and slapping each other's shoulders.

"Who cares who he was," Jacob said.

"I'm so exhausted," Ruth chuckled, "I'm downright silly. All I want to do is just rest my aching bones."

"Agreed, agreed," Jacob shouted. "Come! Make yourselves at home. I have made plans; this will be the best week of your lives. One you will always remember."

Chapter 2

The three boys wanted to start playing immediately, but their parents insisted that they help unload the donkey and take things inside. Then rest was prescribed for the weary family. Later in the evening gifts were presented to Jacob and Matthew. It was customary for guests to bring gifts to the host and his family.

With the formalities over, Rufus asked permission to be excused, followed by Matthew and Alexander. Each parent nodded their consent, for they knew the boys wanted to be by themselves, to trade secrets and just enjoy themselves.

Jacob smiled as the boys scampered outside, then turned to his guests. "You know," he began, "this is the first real happiness the boy has had since his mother died. Thank you, thank you for coming."

Simon had loved his sister, Rachel, very much, and she and Ruth had been very close as sisters-in-law. Her absence was deeply felt. After a period of quiet, Simon said: "It is good that we are here. It is good indeed."

"Enough," said Jacob slapping his hands together. "Enough of sad talk. I have made plans, grand plans that will make your stay here worth every minute." Simon and Ruth sat attentively.

"First thing tomorrow morning we will go to the temple. I have made arrangements for you to meet some of the most important priests and high officials. It was not without some effort mind you. The officials are difficult men to see."

"I know," said Simon. "I appreciate it, and I'm sure it will be an experience I will long remember."

"It sounds fascinating," added Ruth. "And . . . while you're gone I will go to the marketplace . . . Oh, Simon, don't look at me like you look at Rufus. I promise to be thrifty."

"I don't blame you, Simon. I don't think I'd trust her

alone in the marketplace with so much temptation," Jacob teased.

"Nonsense," Ruth pretended to pout. "I know very well how to bargain."

"Yes, I believe she could buy the sword off a Roman in battle if she had a mind to have it as a souvenir," Simon laughed.

The house rang with their laughter. It was good to be with family at such a joyous time.

* * *

The fathers and their sons went to the temple and Ruth finished up the chores and prepared first to stop and visit with her namesake, little Ruth. Perhaps she and Lydia could go to the market together. It was so pleasant being outside; neither too cold nor too hot. A gentle breeze kept the day from being either.

Ruth carefully packed a small gift in her bag and set out for what she knew was going to be a wonderful day.

Along the way to Lydia's house Ruth took in the busy streets of Jerusalem. The streets were far more crowded than the ones back home, and passersby bumped into her and never stopped to ask her pardon. Beggers lined the streets, and small children, dirty and unkempt, fought and swore at each other. This distressed Ruth.

Always there was the presence of Rome. Roman banners flew above certain houses, and often groups of soldiers could be seen walking and milling about. They looked bored and boastfully pushed their authority around; they shoved their way in front of people waiting in line.

Ruth stood in front of Lydia's house and watched a lovely young girl come out. Ruth recognized the girl as Rebecca, the frail and frightened little girl who had approached them on the road pleading for help. She had grown into a lovely girl.

"Rebecca, Rebecca," Ruth called with outstretched arms.

"Oh, Ruth, wife of Simon," Rebecca shouted with

excitement and ran to greet her. "Come inside. Mother will be so happy to see you. And little Ruth, well, you will see for yourself. She has grown."

Inside the meeting of old friends was as it usually is. Each woman gave a full report of the year's events, from scraped knees and lost teeth to the cost of living and recipes. It was just as Ruth had hoped. Her visit was as pleasant as she had dreamed it would be. Little Ruth was growing into a lovely child, and she loved the little pillow Ruth had made her. It was plain to see that Lydia was proud of her daughters.

"Where are Rufus and the boys?" Lydia asked. "We will get a chance to see them before you leave?"

"They are at the temple," Ruth answered. She was about to say something when she noticed the look on Lydia's face. All color had drained from it, and her eyes stared toward the door. Ruth saw in Lydia's eyes something akin to panic. She turned to see what had caused this sudden change in Lydia, and there stood the stranger. Ruth shuddered, and pulled her shawl around her.

"J—J—Judas! Ah, do come in. Forgive me for staring, but I didn't know you were back." Lydia was obviously very nervous and her hands moved from her hair to her face to her lap in jittery motions.

Judas unnerved Ruth, but she managed a courteous smile. He returned it, but it seemed forced and contrived.

"This day has been a day of days," Lydia went on nervously. "First my dear friend Ruth comes to see me, now you Judas. What a pleasant surprise."

At last Judas spoke. "We arrived yesterday. Today I took leave of *them* to come see the family of my brother. I'm sorry if I have caused you an inconvenience. It has been, after all, four years since I've seen you."

His language flowed smoothly as though he were accustomed to using words. Ruth knew that Judas must have been an educated man. But what about him caused Lydia to be so uncomfortable? What about this dark man, who was her kinsman, made her so nervous?

"Forgive me for being rude," Lydia chattered in a high pitch. "Judas, this is Ruth, wife of Simon of Cyrene. They are relatives of Jacob, the Weaver. Ruth, this is my brother-in-law, Judas Iscariot. I—I—I was married to his brother before—before—he died."

Judas and Ruth exchanged greeting nods.

"You say you arrived yesterday?" Ruth inquired, trying to ease the tension that seemed to be ever mounting.

"Yes," answered Judas directly, making no attempt to carry the conversation any further.

"You said 'we.' Did you bring your family?" Ruth persisted. She scolded herself for being like Rufus.

"In a sense," he answered.

Lydia seemed highly agitated at this point. Her hands were visibly shaking. Judas noticed, and Ruth was embarrassed. She knew she should leave and let family members have the privacy they needed. It was rude of her to stay, but something in Lydia's eyes said, "Please don't go." Ruth stayed, although she too was uncomfortable.

Judas inquired about the girls, and Lydia informed him that they were fine and that she had sent them on an errand. Judas asked permission to remain until they came back. "I would like to see the children of my dead brother," he said calmly. "I have never seen the little one. I am sorry I was not able to be with you when you needed me, but you understand my situation."

"We are fine," Lydia almost screamed. "We have managed well. Excuse me, I will get us something to drink." Lydia rose to leave and knocked over the stool. Judas stood to help, but the woman scurried away. "I'm okay," she said. "Really."

Ruth and Judas were left alone.

"Did you run into the crowd?" Ruth finally asked.

"Crowd?"

"Yes, when we arrived yesterday there was a procession led by a man on a donkey and people were waving palm branches and shouting praises to the king. It was so strange."

"Yes, it was strange." Judas looked far away, deep in thought.

"Oh, then you were there?"

"Yes," Judas answered.

"Do you know who the Man . . ."

"Will you please excuse me," Judas said abruptly, standing. "I must go now. Please give Lydia my apologies for leaving. But, I think it's best I go, now."

"But, what . . ." Ruth stammered, confused more now than ever. "You just arrived. Should I tell her you will be returning? When?"

"I'm sorry for ever coming. I shouldn't have. But, I just wanted to see . . ." And he was gone. Ruth sat with her mouth open, looking at the flapping curtain.

Just as he left, Lydia returned with her hands empty.

"Were you standing there all along?" Ruth asked without a second thought. "Why didn't you try to stop him?"

"Good riddance to him," Lydia hissed. "He can only bring trouble to me and my children."

"Lydia!" Ruth exclaimed in surprise. "How can you speak of a kinsman this way? You were married to his brother."

"As different as night is to day. If you knew about him, you would understand my feelings. What I don't understand is how He could have someone like Judas around Him."

"Who?" Ruth asked. "What are you talking about?"

"Listen," Ruth paused as if to gain control of her own emotions as well as give Lydia a chance to compose herself. "Let's start from the beginning. We are old friends. You can trust me, and if I can help I will. You know that."

Lydia's body shook with emotion. "Alright," she began. "I will try to explain." Then she began her story:

"About three years ago, right before my dear, dear husband died, Judas joined a group of fanatics who traveled around with a Nazarene called Jesus. He was a carpenter.

16

"Somehow this Carpenter took it upon Himself to save the world from itself, and He left His trade and set out to change the world. Can you believe—as if that's not enough—this Jesus says He is the . . . the Son of God."

Ruth gasped. "Blasphemy!" she whispered. "Crazy man. Do people believe Him?"

"Oh, but that's just it. Jesus says things that people want to believe. You should hear some of the wild stories many say about Him. Raising people from the dead, and healing the blind and crippled."

"He could be a prophet with powers to do this?"

"No," shouted Lydia, almost hysterical. "He is not a prophet; He is not anything but trouble. He claims He is the Son of God, and people, right here in this city believe that He is the—the Messiah."

"Messiah!" Ruth's eyes were stretched in total disbelief that anyone, anyone in their right mind, would go about telling people they were the Chosen One—unless they were . . . but, no, that was impossible. When the Messiah came, everybody would know it. There would be—could be—no doubt.

"There's more," Lydia continued. "Some actually believe that Jesus has the power to—" at this point Lydia leaned over and whispered in a low voice—"overthrow the Romans!"

"Madness is like a fever, it spreads like fire."

"Anyone who is involved with them will come to no good end. I am frightened. I have heard talk that the authorities are about fed up with Him. I want no part of any of it."

Rebecca returned with little Ruth, and the women changed the subject. Lydia never mentioned Judas' visit to her daughters.

Ruth stood to leave. She hugged her friend of recent years, and left without saying more about the visitor. "I will return later," Ruth said, "when we can talk." Ruth thought on the way home how wonderful that would be. The long-awaited One, actually here on earth? Ruth dismissed the thought. No, if He were the One, there wouldn't be a doubt in anyone's mind.

* * *

Long before she actually entered the house she heard the voices of the men. First she heard her husband's bass tone, then Jacob's shrill tones. Their voices sounded angry.

"What has happened to cause you to be so distressed?" Ruth asked, standing in the doorway.

The talking stopped, and they all looked toward the door to see who was speaking. Then, as though an invisible switch had been thrown, everyone started talking at once.

Jacob stood and called for silence. Rufus was actually jumping up and down with excitement. Alexander, who normally tried to be more mature, was showing signs of impatience.

Jacob cleared his throat. "Never before in my entire life have I seen the likes of what happened today at the temple. As you know," he said, speaking directly to his sister-in-law, "we all went to the temple today. We said our prayers, made our offerings. Simon, here, gave an eloquent prayer of thanksgiving. The priests were very impressed." Ruth cast a look of amazement toward Simon; he was not one known for making public speeches. Jacob continued.

"The temple was full and people were, as usual, buying the necessary doves for sacrifice. Simon, the boys, and I were milling about waiting for our turn to speak with the elders, when out of nowhere—I tell you out of nowhere—this madman came like a wild animal beating the poor fellows out to the temple grounds and turning over their carts and scattering their goods on the ground. Disgraceful. I tell you it was scandalous."

Rufus snickered, and Alexander was hard pressed to keep a solemn face over his uncle's indignation.

Jacob wiped his brow and continued. "And if this isn't bad enough, this wild man, oh Jerusalem has seen some, but this One beats them all. Where was I? Oh, yes, He began

18

to shout things like 'you made My Father's house a den of thieves, and My house should be a house of prayer.'"

Jacob had reached a point where he could go no further. "I am sorry," he said sitting down. "I am deeply sorry that your visit had to be marred by such an outrageous act of blasphemy. But rest assured, this act will not go un-punished."

"Yes, the priests and officials were furious," Alexander added.

"Lord Caiaphas is not one who will let this thing go."

Ruth had sat listening to the story unravel. Bit by bit she put the pieces together. First the procession, the strange Judas, Lydia's account of Jesus, and now the incident at the temple. Ruth felt as though the walls were coming in on her. She looked at her husband and he seemed deep in thought.

"Was this man's name Jesus?" Ruth heard herself asking.

"Yes," Jacob said in a highly agitated voice. "That's the blasphemer's name. He has been preaching about for several years here and there. He's built quite a reputation for Himself and many poor fools have lined themselves up with Him. They call Him the Messiah. Can you believe that?" Jacob was beside himself. He waved his hands and pounded on the table. "Why don't they do something about Him?"

"Yes," said Simon, "why hasn't something been done about Him; if He is allowed to continue . . ."

"He's a slick one," Jacob snapped at the chance to vent his feelings. "He never says or does anything bad enough to be brought before the authorities. He knows the Law and has skillfully managed to alter the Law to fit His needs."

"Tell them the story you told me," encouraged Matthew.

"Ah, yes. This will give you an example of how shrewd He really is. The Law says a woman caught in adultery should be stoned to death. Such an adulteress was found, and she was about to be stoned. Jesus stepped in and saved her. That is against the Law. But, listen how He did it. He

20

said: 'If any one among you is without sin, cast the first stone.' Well, everyone there dropped their stones and fled. He played on the emotions of the people. That's how He operates. This Jesus ..." In midsentence Jacob stopped his narration and looked at Ruth. "How did you know His name?" he asked.

Ruth seemed almost in a trance. "I—I—I went to see my friend Lydia today, and while there, one of the followers of Jesus came to see her ..."

"If she's wise, she will have nothing to do with them," Jacob added.

Ruth went on to tell about Judas and Lydia's story. She was afraid for her friend, and the girls. When her tale ended, Jacob was more convinced than ever that Jesus and His followers were more dangerous than anyone could imagine and they were on a collision course with disaster.

The sun was setting. Alexander leaned over and lit the candles. Long shadows stretched across the floor. The day had been an exhausting day, and they all agreed that they had talked enough about Jesus and His followers for one day.

"No more talk of Jesus," Jacob declared at breakfast the next morning. "Our days will be spent with love and joy with each other's company."

Everyone agreed and Jesus was not mentioned until the morning of His crucifixion.

Chapter 3

"It has happened! It has finally happened!" Ruth heard Jacob shout. Behind him she heard the boys and Simon say something about a crucifixion. She went to the door. Jacob rushed to her. "I tell you it has finally happened."

"What?" Ruth asked, looking from one to the other.

"Jesus," put in Rufus. "We heard He's been tried and found guilty and is going to be put to death by crossifiction!"

"Oh," was all Ruth could let come out of her mouth.

"Hurry," ordered Jacob. "This I must see. I want Matthew to learn firsthand what happens to people who defy the Law and try to pass themselves off as 'Son of God.'"

Simon stood silently by. He didn't say a word, but Ruth could see in his eyes that he was totally convinced that this was not the way to handle the Jesus question. Simon knew the horrors of a crucifixion, and he wasn't too anxious to see it, especially since the Person in question was not really guilty of anything . . .

"May I go?" Rufus pleaded.

But Simon and Ruth were firm, and even Uncle Jacob agreed with them. Crucifixions were not for young children, but Matthew and Alexander were allowed to go. Ruth was not sure about Alexander even though he was 16.

"Please let me go, please. Just this once," Rufus begged. But Simon said no in his final way, and Rufus' hopes were dashed.

The men left.

Rufus tried to entertain himself outside—he was never allowed alone far from the house—but it was no use. So he went inside to talk to his mother about what was happening, perhaps that very moment. As he spoke to Ruth, he became excited. "I heard some people practicing their singing for the religious ceremonies," he told her. "Then I heard some women talking about Jesus," he said.

"They were all going to the crossifiction. They called it
something like that."

While Ruth was not eager to continue on this subject,
she did feel the urge to give her son the correct word, at
least. "It's called a crucifixion," she told her boy. "And it
isn't a very happy occasion. If you think about it from the
point of view of the victims, you might feel ashamed of
your eagerness."

"Oh mother! I'm not anxious for anybody to be hurt.
But since they are going to be, why can't I see it, just like
Alexander?"

"Rufus, do you have any idea what a crucifixion is?"
the woman inquired sadly.

"Sure I do," he went on, in his excited tone. "That's
where they kill a bad man because he did something
terrible." Then he added, again in a pleading way, "We
never get a chance to see one of those at home, Mother.
Please let's both go and watch." He appealed to her to
accompany him because he knew that she would never let
him go by himself. It was his last, desperate hope.

But his mother was firm. "Rufus," she almost scolded,
"you know what your father said. And that's final."

Rufus knew he had lost in his attempt, but he couldn't
take his mind from the subject. "Mother, men *do* those kinds
of things and I'm getting to be a man. If Father saw the
cruki—"

"Crucifixion," she corrected.

"Well, if father sees it, he'll be telling his friends back
home about what happened. That's all I wanted to do, too."

Again, the boy's mother was firm, but now softer in
tone. "Killing is not a subject for children. These men
aren't being put to death for anybody's entertainment. You
make it almost sound like some kind of show or
something."

"Mother, how come they are putting Jesus to death?"
he asked.

Ruth put her work down for a moment, wiped her
hands, and tousled Rufus' hair. Gently she responded to

the boy. "There has been so much talk about this Jesus since we arrived. There are so many contradictions about Him. Some say He spoke of love and peace, that surely couldn't be a crime. Others say He was blasphemous and a rabble-rouser. It's all so confusing to me I don't know what to think. But I'm sure He had a fair trial, and He offered His defense."

"Well, I heard some of the talk, and it isn't very clear to me either."

"Yes," Ruth went on rather sadly, "it is too bad it had to come to this end. Surely they could have found a way to handle Him other than . . ." She went back to her cooking chores, awaiting the next barrage of questions.

She did not have to wait long. "Suppose He was the Son of God? What do you think He'll do? Maybe He'll put up a fight." And as Ruth was preparing to reply, Rufus asked other questions, "What if He has an army waiting to attack?"

Ruth stood listening to her son. She remembered what Lydia had said about Judas saying Jesus was going to lead an army into Jerusalem. "No, if this were true, then why did He preach about love, even loving your enemy? And as for an army, they would have moved before now."

"But just suppose," said Rufus.

But Ruth didn't want to suppose. "Am I frightened?" she thought. But before she could begin to answer, Rufus was off to another question, "How do they do it?"

"That's enough," Ruth said strongly. "Please go outside now and get me some wood for the cooking fire. At least you can make yourself useful while you are waiting so eagerly to hear about all this bad business."

Ruth thought about the crucifixion. Was it the end of Jesus? Somehow she wasn't so sure. She was worried about Lydia.

Chapter 4

Rufus was not exactly moving with great speed. He ambled towards the woodpile even sadder than he was before. He kicked at a stone and stubbed his sandal on the ground and scraped several toes. The boy jumped around but was too unhappy to howl, and finally just settled on one end of the stacked logs to gather his thoughts before going on to gather the wood for his mother.

He had just sat down when he heard the men coming home. Curiously, Rufus froze, stayed sitting where he was, and just watched as the figures began to emerge in front of a nearby house. Alexander and Matthew came first, talking quietly. Jacob and Simon, the two fathers, were totally silent. Each man seemed to be putting one foot in front of the other in an almost forced way, as if they had to think about walking rather than doing it naturally. And the faraway expressions on their faces were immediately noticeable. Rufus became puzzled. Should he have gone or not, he wondered.

Rufus did not want to ask his brother or his cousin about what happened. That would only make them feel too big and important. His all-of-a-sudden plan was to go into the house and hope that his mother would ask his father how things went, and then he'd get all of the information he'd need to relay to his farm pals.

Rufus quickly grabbed some twigs, a few thicker pieces, and finally a couple of logs and headed for his mother's side. "They're back," he said, as casually as he could.

"Oh, I'm glad," Ruth said. "I'm glad the whole nasty situation is over. Let's get them a little something to eat. Maybe what they saw wasn't too upsetting."

In walked the sons first. Ruth instantly noticed that they were not their boisterous selves. Even Rufus could see that the boys were far from being proud about where they'd been. He tried to read the meaning of their faces. Was it shame? Was it guilt?

Ruth rushed to the curtain and looked toward the men, still a few yards from the house. "Simon looks terrible," she said, talking to herself. "And Jacob . . ." her voice trailed off as they came nearer.

As the men entered, Jacob could see that Ruth was stunned. Understanding that Simon was not going to say anything right then—was not able to say anything—Jacob thought that he might say a little for Ruth's sake. "We saw the crucifixions," he told her. "We ran into their procession on the way to the hill where they were to die. It was not pleasant."

And then they all were silent for what seemed to be a very long time.

Matthew knew that the adults had some important matters to discuss and wished to do so privately. He suggested that the boys go out and play. Alexander was puzzled by this invitation but then caught on. He knew that his cousin was right and admired him for his insight. "C'mon Ruf," Alexander said. "Let's go play a game!"

But Rufus wasn't about to go outside. He'd been waiting a long time and there was no way he was going outside now. Alexander just snatched Rufus' arm in that no nonsense way he sometimes had, and Rufus realized that he had no choice. "You'll find out later," Alexander whispered to Rufus. "Come now!"

"Simon, I've never seen you like this. What's the matter?" Ruth said.

Simon spoke to her in a dull, flat voice, his mind still somewhere else—out *there*. "They made me carry His cross."

His wife was horrified. "You? Why you? Why would they shame an innocent man?" Then she turned to Jacob to continue her questioning. "Why a stranger?" she asked.

Again, silence.

Finally, Jacob spoke. He sat down on a chair, clearly exhausted, yet his body could not be still. His fingers locked and unlocked, balled into fists, opened, closed, as if they were searching to find words and meaning just like

Rufus was. "It's *because* he is a stranger," Jacob found himself explaining, not sure if he'd said too much or too little.

"I don't understand you," Ruth responded. "There's a tradition of hospitality that we all believe in, isn't there? If you come to visit us—" But the woman caught herself immediately. She was practically scolding her brother-in-law and saying, we wouldn't let this happen to you if you came to visit us—we know our manners. And this is not what Ruth wanted to do. It was not her intention at all to attack Jacob. She was just hurt and confused.

Jacob seemed to understand all of this, without Ruth even apologizing. "Jesus has become so controversial, and since it is shameful to carry a cross, the soldiers didn't want to start any trouble by picking one of the people from this area. These people all have friends and there could have been a real riot around here. Some of the local people really hated Jesus, but they hate the Roman soldiers even more. Well, the soldiers know that, and while they wouldn't mind knocking a few heads, they have orders not to unless they just can't help it. So they knew by the color of Simon's black skin that he isn't from here, and they picked on him. They forced him," Jacob continued. "He refused to take up the cross but they made him do it. They might have beaten Simon if he had refused their orders."

"Oh Simon!" was all that Ruth could say. Her husband did not look up from the space on the floor at which he was staring.

Jacob felt that he had to say more. He went over to the fire, as if to check on what was cooking, though when he looked he never even noticed the bread. "I've never been so ashamed. It is disgraceful to treat a visitor to our city like this. It is personally disgraceful to have it happen to *my* guest, to *my* brother-in-law." After a moment Jacob added: "I would protest to the authorities after the holidays. But what good will that do? Even if the Imperial Officer in charge of the troops here does agree with me—and who knows if he will or not—what can he do? Send a message saying he's sorry and it won't happen again? Of course it won't happen again. Does he think Simon'll ever want to visit us, ever?" There was a longer pause this time, and then Jacob finished by saying, "Anyway, we left early, before they actually crucified them. As soon as Simon helped get His cross up the hill, we chose not to stay."

"Well, Simon," the woman insisted, trying to be of comfort, "everyone surely knew that you weren't a criminal of any kind."

But Simon was not to be comforted. He turned to her by way of anxious explanation. "That's the worst part of all. Jesus wasn't a thief." Then Simon's mind was gone again, to the streets, to Golgotha, to the soldiers, to the Victim.

"The crowd was awful to Him. Mind you, I wasn't a Jesus follower. I believe the Man was mad, but seeing Him there . . . they had beaten Him, you know . . . as a grown man, I felt fear for the first time."

Simon's reply was simple: "He certainly wasn't afraid when we saw Him."

Again there was a silence in the house—a silence Jacob felt was awkward. He felt Simon would probably like to be alone with Ruth for a time and so looked for an excuse to leave. Picking up a huge earthenware container, he announced that he was going outdoors: "I'll go to the well for some water. I also want to see how the boys are doing." Then he exited quietly.

Alone with his beloved wife, Simon was able to say words which he had held back because he knew they might hurt his brother-in-law. "I wish we had never come." Then he said it in another way: "Why did we have to run into that terrible procession?"

The woman came near her troubled husband, took his hand, and tried to soothe him: "Simon, don't let Jacob hear you say that. He has been so generous to let us come here during the holy days. He loves us, Simon, and we mustn't hurt him. Please, Simon."

But the man was unable to raise his spirits. "You don't understand. Everyone laughed at me. Jacob saw that. He

saw what a fool I became in their minds."

Ruth's eyes had tears in them. She couldn't bear the image of a large group of people mocking her husband, jeering him. It was so unfair. Simon had never been mean to anyone. Everyone who knew Simon liked him because of his kindness, his generosity, his willingness to sacrifice for his family and friends. How unfair indeed.

Then Simon elaborated. "Jacob didn't laugh, of course, and neither did Jesus. But Jesus did more than just not laugh." Simon turned to his wife and held her closely. "You should have seen the way He looked at me. There was something in His eyes, something in His smile. Yes, when I took up His cross on my shoulders He actually smiled. Not the grin of a madman, but a smile of understanding; as though He was trying to say thank you. That's the only way I can explain it. A kind of fullness of eternity."

The woman thought about Jesus for a moment. "Son of God? Simon, He wasn't—He wasn't, was He?"

He answered in an almost ghostly voice: "I don't know what to think." And then, as if to emphasize his dilemma, he said again, "I just don't know what to believe."

Alexander and Matthew had told Rufus the entire story. Rufus sat with his head down listening to the boys tell about the shame his father had suffered.

When Rufus lifted his head, he said with tears in his eyes. "Why? Why our father?"

Suddenly the sky turned as dark as night and the winds blew, forcing everyone inside.

Chapter 5

It was evening and the Sabbath had begun. Slowly and methodically the family went through the rituals of the Passover celebration. The candles were lit and Jacob in a gesture of compassion offered Simon the privilege of leading the prayers. Simon refused, but after gentle persuasion from his family, he accepted. He spoke the words of the ancient prayers with such emotion that everyone, even young Rufus, who frequently daydreamed during the celebrations, was deeply touched.

They ate and talked about first one thing, then another, each person careful not to mention the events of the day. Rufus guarded his tongue, because he felt for his father.

Jacob seemed to be the most ill at ease. He had so hoped for his family's visit to be a good one. He studied the faces of his guests and found that their eyes were full of distress. What could he do? He heard himself chattering aimlessly about trivial things, until finally the conversation fell into silence.

It was Simon who spoke first: "Will they bury Him?"

There was no question as to whom he was talking about. It was as though someone had released a great gust of wind that was being held against its will.

"I'm sure they will bury Him; He had family I'm sure, or the men who followed Him will see to it," Ruth said quietly.

"I must know more about Him," Simon said softly, as though he weren't really speaking to be heard.

Jacob stood abruptly. "That's it!" he said. "That's it! We need to find out everything we can. We went about it all wrong. We never really—well, I was never really willing to learn both sides of the Jesus question. Perhaps I was wrong, and I will be the first to admit that. I don't yet believe He was the Son of God, but I don't believe He was as bad as they say He was either."

His guests remained silent. It was Jacob who had been

so against Jesus, but now he was willing to at least hear more about the Man.

For the first time in hours Simon seemed to stir. "Yes," he said, "that makes sense. Whatever we learn, it will help me to at least understand all that happened."

"Tomorrow I will go to the temple again and see what I can find out," said Jacob.

Ruth said, "And I will go to Lydia's again and learn what I can. Her brother-in-law, Judas, might be able to shed some light on the subject."

"May I go?" Rufus asked, looking first to Simon then his mother. Ruth nodded her consent, and Simon agreed.

The older boys spoke up. "We will help too," said Matthew. "Several of my friends know about Jesus," he confessed, looking at Jacob. "I never mentioned it before, because you were so against Him, father. But, maybe I can find out something."

Jacob placed his arm on his son's shoulder. "I am not the wisest man in the world, but I am willing to admit that I might be wrong. We shall see . . . go and find out what you can."

It was agreed, then, that they would all find out as much as they could about Jesus and His followers. They all knew, too, that what they were about to do could bring about trouble for Jacob and his son. Ruth remembered the fear of Lydia. She warned them all to be very careful.

*   *   *

The next day was unseasonably cool and heavy clouds hung over the city. Great gusts of wind swept the loose garments of the people on the streets. Ruth and Rufus trudged along, turning their shoulders to the wind. Once the mother had to lean against a wall to protect herself from the wind. She pulled her shawl over her face to shield her eyes from the dust and sand.

"Alms," a beggar pleaded pitifully. "Alms for the poor!"

Ruth dropped a coin in his cup and moved away quickly.

A Roman soldier was coming out of a house dragging a man by the arm. The man begged and pleaded for mercy.

"Dog!" the soldier smirked. "You aren't fit to breathe the air." The man whimpered like a puppy and fell on his knees. From behind the curtain of the house, Ruth could see the eyes of his family watching in silent fear.

"Please," Ruth interrupted. "What is it the man has done to deserve such treatment?"

The soldier released his victim, who scampered quickly to the safety of his house. The soldier menacingly approached Ruth. The woman stood frozen in fear. She had heard of Roman cruelty, but never before had she been confronted with it. Rufus moved between his mother and the soldier. The blow came without warning, but it flung the child to the ground. Ruth watched in horror.

"You touch my mother, and . . ."

"And what, little flea?" laughed the soldier. He reached out to grab Ruth.

"Stop!" a voice commanded. The soldier snapped to attention. "Is this the conduct of a Roman soldier?" Another Roman, obviously of a higher rank, appeared from the shadows, his red cape flapping in the wind.

"No sir," said the soldier. "This woman and her son were interfering in my duties."

Rufus had managed to get to his feet, none the worse from the blow he had taken on the head. He took his place beside his mother and slipped his hand in her hand. His posture suggested that if need be he would defend his mother to the death. Ruth felt that the officer was not to be feared, and squeezed Rufus' hand as a signal to relax.

"Do your duties include beating small boys and bothering women on the streets?" questioned the officer.

"No sir. I was arresting a man for . . ."

"What man? I see no man," the officer snapped.

The curtain of the house flapped in the wind.

The soldier was embarrassed. "No sir. The man is in that house," he said pointing toward the house where the man had been dragged out. "As I was taking him into custody this . . . this woman came up and interfered."

The officer looked at Ruth, a small woman in stature, and certainly no physical match for a Roman soldier.

"And what did she do?" the officer continued. "Knock you to the ground? Take your sword?"

"No sir," the soldier said quietly. "She asked me what the man had done."

"Oh, I see," said the officer. "She obstructed justice by asking you what the man had done. And for *this* you struck her son, and . . ."

"No sir, I was just going to warn them."

"I think enough has been said and done. I get the picture very clearly. I will handle this myself. You return to the barracks, and we will discuss this in more detail later."

The soldier looked toward the house, then walked quickly away.

The wind whipped at their garments. Ruth sighed and Rufus relaxed his tense muscles. The officer waited until his man had rounded the corner, then spoke to Ruth.

"I am very sorry for the conduct of my soldier. Please, if I can be of assistance in getting you somewhere safely, I will."

Ruth found her tongue, then spoke quickly. "I had no intentions of obstructing justice. It was just that the man was being treated so badly. For all I know the man may have been guilty of some crime, but where I'm from a man is innocent until found guilty. Are you going to look into it?"

"I think not," said the officer, looking toward the house. The curtain moved ever so slightly. "The situation here is that the soldier probably took an interest in one of the man's lovely daughters. When the old man would not allow it, the soldier simply invented some charge against the father to get him out of the house and leave the women unprotected. It is quite common."

"But won't he come back?" Rufus added.

"I think not," the officer spoke with assurance. "I will see to it." The officer seemed to be speaking not to Ruth and Rufus, but to the people behind the curtain in the house. From inside they heard a praise of thanks and shouts of gladness. The officer smiled and Ruth smiled at the officer. She liked him. He was not like any Roman she had ever known or had heard about.

Rufus liked the Roman too. His easy manner and gentle voice were in contrast to his masculine frame.

"We are going to my friend's house just a few streets away," Ruth said, beginning to walk.

"I will see that you get there," the officer said, falling in beside her.

"Are you a general?" asked Rufus.

"No, not yet," he smiled. "I'm a captain, and I just arrived here a week ago from Rome. It's been quite a week," he remarked thoughtfully.

"We're here just for the week. We go home to Cyrene in a day or two," Rufus chattered on, eyeing the sword. He wanted so badly to touch it. He wanted to ask questions about war, and fighting, but he knew better than to do that with his mother there.

"Cyrene," he said thoughtfully again.

Ruth answered this time. "We are visiting relatives here for the Passover week."

"I trust your stay has been a pleasant one up until now?"

"Great!" Rufus answered quickly. He wanted to go into details, but thought better of it. Ruth didn't answer. It would not have been a lie to say her stay had been nothing short of disastrous, but to say it would call for explanation.

Their pace was slow, seemingly set by the Roman. He seemed to want the walk to take longer. He chatted freely with Rufus, answering all sorts of questions about Rome and faraway places. Ruth remained silent most of the way.

"There . . . there is the house," she said. "I think we can make it from here. Thank you . . . I'm sorry, what is your name?"

The face of the Roman had become somber and still; the smile had faded. "Is that the house you are going to visit?"

Ruth wanted to say no, and run away with Rufus as fast as she could. But, instead, she nodded her head. Let the worst come, she told herself.

"Tell me," the Roman said with urgency in his voice, "is your visit by any remote chance regarding Jesus of Nazareth?"

Her eyes searched for some hidden reason for his question. Why did he want to know? What did he know of Jesus?

"Why do you ask?" Ruth tactfully evaded the answer she wasn't sure was safe to give. For once Rufus felt the potential danger in their situation and kept quiet.

"I'm sorry," the Roman said hitting his forehead with the palm of his hand. "I forgot that Jerusalem is occupied and we Romans are considered the enemy. I had no idea my question would set you ill at ease. Let's start over again. My name is Flavius Claudius, captain of the Roman guard."

"I am Ruth, wife of Simon of Cyrene. This is Rufus, our son."

They exchanged nods.

"Now," began Flavius, "I'll try to explain briefly why I asked you if you were visiting this house regarding Jesus." Flavius looked around and escorted Ruth and Rufus to a nearby bench where they could sit down. The winds had subsided some, but they huddled together because of the dampness that seemed to penetrate their very bones.

Flavius continued his explanation. "You see, when I arrived here last week, the city was in an uproar about a carpenter from Nazareth who claimed to be a Messiah. You probably understand what that means more than I do."

"It seems the poor fellow ran afoul of the authorities, and He was sentenced to death by the Governor. I was at the trial. Jesus offered no defense. He said nothing. Nothing. Pilate would have set Him free, but the citizenry asked that he free Barabbas instead of Jesus. Strange. I was placed in charge of His crucifixion."

Ruth closed her eyes to block out the memory of what

she knew of that crucifixion and the part her husband had played in it.

"I am a soldier," Flavius was saying. "I face my enemy and he has a sword and we fight to the end. That is honorable, to me.

"I take no pride in crucifixion, even when it is justly deserved, and I feel that Jesus was not guilty of any crime that merited death. That was yesterday," he sighed. "Do you remember when it got dark as night in midday and the earth trembled?"

Ruth, who remained speechless, simply nodded. How will I ever forget, she thought. Rufus was fidgeting and trying hard to contain himself. He wanted to speak out and tell all he knew and compare stories with Flavius.

"I was up there," Flavius said, looking toward Golgotha. "I saw it all. I saw Him suffer and die. Do you know He never mumbled a curse or uttered anything defiant. He asked for water. But the one thing I remember He said was 'Forgive them, Father, for they don't know what they're doing.' Something like that. He told one of the thieves next to Him that he was forgiven and that he would be with Him in Paradise."

Ruth tried to still her body that shook either from the chill or some unseen force. This whole situation was so strange. Here she was sitting on a bench in Jerusalem talking to a Roman soldier about Jesus, a Man who claimed He was the Son of God. It was unreal. But why did he connect Lydia's house with Jesus, she thought. Her eyes glanced toward the house.

Flavius looked too. Then he spoke again: "I wanted to know more about this Jesus. I feel deep down inside me that what I did, or was forced to do, was wrong. Do you know what I mean?"

"Oh yes, more than you will know," said Ruth, thinking about the feelings of her husband.

"Anyway, I checked around all day yesterday and half of today. I found out that Jesus had 12 men who traveled with Him. One was named Simon Peter from Capernaum;

there was James and John. Another was named Judas Iscariot. I haven't been able to locate anyone who knows where these men are!"

"Weren't they at the crucifixion?"

"No, not that I know of. His mother claimed His body and He was buried. It seems once their Leader was killed the others scattered."

"You mean they deserted Him when He needed them?" Rufus said, rather disgusted.

"Well, that's what it seems. I can't find any of them."

"Some friends," Rufus said and kicked a stone as far as he could.

Flavius looked at Ruth and his face was still and calm. "You knew Him, didn't you?" he asked.

"No," Ruth stated.

Flavius believed her.

"Just this morning I heard that one of His followers, Judas, hanged himself this morning. One of the guards said that he had been found and that they were looking for someone to claim the body. They seemed to have found through city registration that a woman living here in the city is his sister-in-law, Lydia. She lives there in that house. I was coming to speak with her about . . . well, you know the rest.

Ruth clutched her shawl and gasped. "Dead," she whispered, "by his own hands?"

"Griefstricken probably. It seems His followers were as loyal as His enemies. Some of them at least."

"We had never heard of Jesus until we came here— we've also been here only a week. My husband saw Him at the temple, and I met Judas only briefly at my friend Lydia's house." She chose not to tell of Simon being forced by the Romans to carry Jesus' cross. It might cause Flavius embarrassment, and he had been very kind. "I am concerned about Lydia," Ruth said pensively. "She seemed so frightened about Jesus and Judas."

It was Rufus' time to speak. "Mother," he said softly,

"maybe Lydia might know something that will be of help to us. Maybe if we went in . . ."

"Dare we go in now?" Ruth sighed. "I don't think I could handle it at this time."

"And my presence wouldn't help much now either," said Flavius. "A Roman asking questions might give her cause to be frightened."

"I don't think she knows anything," Ruth said, holding her arms to stop the involuntary shaking. "I think we should go and return later."

"Come," said Flavius, "let me see you home. The weather is changing." The walk home was faster and each one—Ruth, Flavius, and Rufus—seemed absorbed in their own private thoughts, but they were all thinking about the Carpenter from Nazareth.

"May I come and speak to you and your husband later?" Flavius asked abruptly.

"If you think it will do you any good," answered Ruth. "We know so little ourselves. Besides, this is not my home. Jacob would have to be consulted before I could invite you to come . . . but," she added quickly, seeing his disappointment, "if I ask him, I am sure he will agree."

"I will come for you at the barracks," Rufus offered, beaming at the prospect of actually seeing a Roman barracks.

Flavius smiled. "You do that, little friend. I will be waiting." He looked at Ruth, "See what you can do," he said softly. "I really must find some answers."

Chapter 6

"A Roman soldier!" shouted Jacob. "In my house!" he continued softer, "Never!"

"But he was there," added Rufus. "He was at Golgotha, and he is just as troubled about what he had to do as father is. Please, Uncle Jacob, let him come."

"You are not old enough to understand," answered Jacob stubbornly. "Romans are . . ."

"People!" Simon interjected. "The boy speaks with wisdom beyond his years. Listen to him Jacob."

"How can you be so concerned of Roman feelings after what they forced you to do, Simon?"

Ruth retorted quickly. "What happened to Simon may not yet be understood. If Jesus was the Son of God, then it would have been an honor for Simon to have helped Him. Especially since Flavius said His followers all deserted Him, or most of them at least. Judas is dead by his own hands, and . . ." The tears came uncontrollably. The strain of the last few days had taken their toll, and Ruth couldn't stand it any more.

"Alright, alright," Jacob threw up his hands. "I see I've lost. Tears I can't handle. He can come; he can come!"

"Another thing," Simon started as if continuing from only a moment before—the flood waters of his mind were bursting forth—"those other two men were carrying their crosses without too much trouble." Ruth looked puzzled at Simon. What was the point of his remark, she wondered. "Well, you know I'm as strong as the next man." He wasn't bragging, just stating a fact. "But Jesus' cross was very heavy. I couldn't keep up with the others, especially on the uphill part." His voice trailed off and he became silent again.

* * *

It was evening; Rufus, Alexander, and Matthew had been sent to get Flavius.

Jacob smiled, but he wasn't in a happy mood. Simon's

troubles weighed more heavily on him. Jacob stepped outside to get a breath of air and examine the sky.

Just then he saw a person coming up the street. He was a stranger, unknown to any of them.

The man appeared to be looking for something—or perhaps it was for someone. Jacob asked the stranger, who was obviously poor, judging by his clothing, if he could be of any help. "Thank you, sir," said the unknown man. "I wonder if you could tell me which house the Cyrenian is visiting, I have need to speak with him."

Jacob became immediately wary. Because of the events of the past few days he wasn't sure if he wanted to tell anyone about Simon's whereabouts. "Have the Roman soldiers sent you to inquire about him?" Jacob asked with suspicion.

At first the stranger was puzzled by Jacob's question and he remained silent. Then he gradually came to realize the basis of Jacob's mistrust. "No, no, I assure you," he replied, "I am not a spy or a betrayer. One traitor in our midst is terrible enough." Jacob wanted to ask for an explanation but held his tongue. "No," he then continued, "I am one of the followers of Jesus. My name is Thomas, and I wish sincerely to meet the man called Simon, who has come here from far away and who has taken the burden of our Master's cross upon his back as none of us has ever done. Please, do you know where he is?"

Feeling overwhelmed by the situation, Jacob did not know what to do. Should he believe the man? Ordinarily, he would have trusted the stranger. Flavius was coming, a Roman captain. Wouldn't this make for an awkward situation, he thought.

After a long pause, Jacob decided that in any event he would not lie—nothing is ever gained from doing that. So he told the stranger to wait. "Simon is here," he went on. "He is my brother-in-law and my guest. I shall ask him if he wishes to see you. If he says no then I shall have to ask you to respect the privacy of my home and to leave the man in peace."

The response was straightforward and simple: "You know that we Jews are firm believers in the sanctity of a hearth. I come not as an invader but as a friend and seeker. I shall be grateful if you will tell the Cyrenian why it is that I have come."

Jacob was reassured by the man's words and by his humble yet firm attitude. He was still puzzled by what this visit might mean, but he told Thomas to wait and he would bring Simon's reply.

When he went inside, Jacob had no doubt that Simon would choose to see the visitor. Jacob ushered in the man.

The stranger had eyes only for the cross carrier. "Thank you for seeing me, Simon. I am called Thomas, one of Jesus' disciples, and I have need to speak with you."

Another mystery had arisen. Simon inquired in a low, steady, and untrusting voice: "How do you know my name?"

Jacob explained that when the soldiers had forced Simon to shoulder the cross, he, Jacob, had given them Simon's name and country. "I thought that if I mentioned your name and proved to them you were a stranger, they would let you go, Simon. It turns out that I was completely wrong, that it was a stranger that they wanted all along. Simon, I'm sorry but you see that I—"

"Please, Jacob, that isn't important," Simon interrupted. "What is it you want of me, Thomas?"

"The cross, Simon, the cross brought me here. There are things which I cannot understand about it. There are things that I feel ought to be more clear. They are so important."

"And you come to me?" Simon nearly shouted. "How do you think I feel? I'm not only puzzled by it, the whole thing frightens me. I can't help you. I need you to help me!"

The disciple understood. "Perhaps we can aid each other," he offered.

Though he felt that he would disappoint the man, Simon was now coming to feel a kinship with Thomas. There was comfort in knowing that others were almost as

overwhelmed as Simon was by the whole crucifixion episode.

Again, yet another pause took place. Jacob filled this one by suggesting that they all take chairs. Simon slumped into one and then Thomas went to stand beside him, eager not to miss anything which the Cyrenian might have to say. Ruth said she'd get them all something warm to drink.

It was at this point that Jacob spoke again. Outwardly he appeared quite calm, but inwardly he was all atremble, somehow aware that a momentous instance in history might well be taking place under his roof. "Forgive me," he said, "but it appears that there are many difficult things to understand about this Friend of yours. Many of those who heard Him preach have wondered how it is that He claims to be the Son of God." Jacob stopped, not wishing to offend, but having said this much, he had to go on. "If He is the Son of God, why did He die? And there are other things too I'd like to know about. There is a quality to His stories, His parables, which have left many to wonder. Sometimes they seem like useless stories. Yet at other times they are almost beautifully mysterious."

The disciple remained silent, thoughtful. So Jacob went on like an ox pulling his plow through loose topsoil. "I heard that He said unless we became like a little child we would not go to heaven. That isn't very easy to figure out. Then He told a story which another friend told me about, in which a Samaritan, of all people, rescued a common stranger. But I could see the meaning of that story, it made sense. There was a real lesson in that for me."

Simon wished Jacob would stop now. He was going on too long. He looked at Jacob with a glance that was kind but communicated his strong wish. Jacob, somewhat embarrassed, stilled his tongue.

Chapter 7

The curtains flapped and standing in the doorway was Flavius in full Roman attire. Thomas never flinched; never batted an eye.

Ruth rushed toward him. "You came."

"Was there any doubt that I wouldn't?"

"No," she said. Then turning to Thomas she began a nervous introduction. "Thomas, there is no need to fear; Flavius is a Roman, but he has come to learn more about Jesus."

Thomas looked at Flavius with some measure of doubt. Flavius seemingly read his mind and responded.

"I was responsible for His death."

"We all were," answered Thomas.

"Maybe, but I was in charge of the execution. I feel I killed an innocent man. I know nothing of your God; I know nothing of your religion whatsoever. But I do know that something—something was terribly wrong. I am accustomed to killing and death. That is the nature of my profession, but Jesus' death . . . well it seemed so pointless."

"Maybe," said Thomas looking at the Roman with compassion. Thomas welcomed him to join them and Jacob relaxed.

Questions began, first from Simon directed to Thomas, then from Thomas to Flavius, and on and on.

The follower of Jesus explained. "Jesus told us all to take up our crosses and follow Him. That seems easy enough to understand." He noticed that everyone in the room seemed to question his meaning, so he went on in explanation. "The road to eternal life is a long and difficult one. But if that was all He meant, then saying it would have been enough."

Again Thomas went deeper into the recesses of his mind to find some conclusion to where this line of thought would lead. Then he resumed his words. "Jesus always spoke in parables, stories with a meaning. Could His death on the cross be yet another parable? A symbol?"

Thomas continued, "One way that this makes sense to me is to think of the cross as representing our sins. If I carry my personal sins, my own failings . . ."

"How do you mean that?" Ruth asked, eager for an explanation.

"I'm not sure," was the disciple's humble reply. "But let me try to explore this out loud a little more deeply. If each one of us carries our own sins, then why would the Son of God carry a cross, too? He would be beyond sin. But of course the whole purpose of a Redeemer would be to relieve us of the burden of our sins. His cross would be a kind of totality of all of our crosses. He would lift the weight from our backs."

Then, pronouncing every word as if it were the most important he had ever uttered, Simon said very slowly, "His cross . . . was . . . so . . . heavy."

"Exactly, exactly," muttered Thomas, who was now seeing more possibilities over which to ponder. Everyone was hushed. Ruth was weeping, but silently. Rufus was rather frightened, but he did not make a sound.

Suddenly, Flavius sat erectly. "I have listened to all you've said. Very little of it makes sense to me. I need more concrete evidence, facts. It's very Roman of me I know, but I just can't tell. There is something missing, a link, a tie-in."

"I feel that way too," said Jacob, almost ashamed that he could agree with a Roman, especially on something as personal as this. "As you know, I was not a believer in Jesus. I still have doubts about His being the Christ."

"I doubted too, at first," said Thomas. "But after knowing Him, seeing His works, hearing His words, I've never doubted since that Jesus was the Savior. He came, gave us His wonderful message, and just as He told us, He died and is now in heaven with his Father. That I will never doubt."

Ruth spoke, "We all have our doubts. Jesus is so new to

us. To Flavius it is even more difficult. You had the benefit of knowing Him; we at least knew of the prophecies of the One who would come."

"Tell me the prophecies," said Flavius. "I need to know."

Between Ruth and Jacob, Thomas and Simon they each told the story of the Coming according to the prophecies, and Thomas told of his travels with Jesus over the last few years.

Flavius sat enthralled.

Thomas stood. "It is time for me to leave. Thank you all for your kindness to me in allowing me to come into your home. I hope we will meet again soon." It seemed he wanted to say something more to Simon on parting, but no words came to him.

Chapter 8

After Thomas left, the rest of the group moved about in search of some relief from the long hours of conversation. Flavius began to feel the strain and stood to leave. "I, too, will take my leave," he said politely.

"I hope you have learned something that will help you," Ruth said, escorting him to the door.

"A little," he said sadly. "Oh, there was one thing I did learn," he said, remembering something he felt he should have mentioned earlier. "I learned why Judas hanged himself."

"Please, what is it?"

"I'm afraid it isn't too pleasant," Flavius said, lowering his voice. "It seems Judas sold out Jesus for money. He was paid to identify Jesus, so that He would be arrested. It appears that when Judas found himself an outcast for what he had done, he hanged himself. It is very strange indeed. I don't understand how a man like Jesus could inspire people who held Him in such high regard like Thomas, and then at the same time there would be others who would betray Him for money, like Judas."

"Poor Lydia," was all Ruth could say. "I must go see her tomorrow."

Flavius thanked Simon and Jacob for allowing him to come.

"Flavius, you are a Roman," said Jacob, "and I don't think you truly understand what your coming here really means to you or to us. A week ago all of this would have been impossible, but things have changed. A Jesus follower and a Roman, both in my house at the same time . . . Things do change." Jacob extended his hand, and they clasped their arms in a genuine shake of friendship.

Simon stood and extended his hand. Flavius took it and replied: "Simon, you carried His cross, and I put Him to death; we can only wonder why we were chosen for the tasks . . ."

"Chosen?" was Simon's reply.

"Yes, I can't help but believe that we were chosen, Simon. We had no choice in what we did."

"No choice? No choice . . ." Simon again slumped to his chair and stared toward the floor.

Flavius left without further word.

* * *

The next day, the first day of the week, Ruth went to see Lydia, who was beside herself with shame and worry. Ruth tried to console Lydia as best she could, but she, herself, had been so drained from the past few days that she had very little consolation to offer Lydia.

"Judas was a traitor," Lydia wailed. "He sold his Friend's life for thirty, dirty pieces of silver; the price of a slave. I knew that Judas was a good-for-nothing, but this . . . He has shamed us all. He has shamed us."

"Judas will suffer for his wrongdoings, but you, Lydia, have done no wrong. You cannot personally be blamed." Ruth couldn't say that with as much conviction as she wanted. Why did she feel like they, all of them, had in some way been guilty . . . guilty of what? betrayal? denial? not believing when they had the chance? refusing to see what was so plain? Had they all been Judases?

* * *

The next morning the family bid their farewells and set out for the gates of Jerusalem. It was very different from the day they had arrived. There were no great expectations of happy times; no joy of seeing old friends and family. Instead, they made their way through the city toward the gates in silence.

"It's a beautiful day," Alexander exclaimed. The overcast of the past few days had moved and the sun was shining brilliantly.

"It is a beautiful day," said Simon. "It's as though . . . well, in a strange way, it's as though the sun seems happy."

The family smiled and moved on.

They were well out of the city when they heard the shout. Simon halted the donkey and turned to see a horse being ridden by a Roman. The rider was waving his hands and shouting for Simon to halt.

"It is Flavius," Simon said amazed. "He seems . . .

"Simon of Cyrene," Flavius was shouting. "Stop! Stop! I have news you must hear!"

Flavius almost fell off his horse when he reached the surprised family. He was out of breath and rambling on about "news." What news was so important that he would ride at such a pace for Simon to hear? After a moment to catch his breath, he began his narration:

"The key, the missing link . . . it happened. It happened!"

"What? What are you talking about? It has to do with Jesus?" Simon was getting anxious.

"Guards were posted at Jesus' tomb," Flavius began breathlessly, "but, Jesus is not in His tomb any longer. He has risen. He has risen from the dead!"

"He is mad," whispered Alexander to Rufus.

"No," said Rufus. "Look at his eyes. They are not the eyes of a madman. I think he speaks the truth."

"When was this?" Ruth asked.

"Yesterday. The third day after His death. The guards reported that the sealed stone rolled away by some mighty force, and when they looked inside there was no one there. Foul play was suspected, but I checked it out thoroughly. The guards had not been bribed. The look on their faces was that of real fear. I don't care what they say, I know that it is true. Jesus is the Son of God, and He lives."

"Yes," said Simon. "He conquered death. He died on a cross, suffered like a man, but then He rose from the dead as only the Son of God could do. It all fits together, now!"

Flavius continued. The family sat beneath a boulder and listened to the excited Roman. "I had my doubts at first. But, I found Thomas. He and the others who followed Him have seen Him. Thomas said that he had insisted

upon touching the wounds in Jesus' hands and feet. Thomas was so ashamed of doubting."

"We all doubted," said Ruth. "We all did."

"That was proof enough for me," Flavius went on. "I know that Thomas would not lie about a thing like that. I went to Jacob and told him, and he has gone now to find Thomas and the others. I came to find you."

Ruth looked at the Roman, her sons, and her husband.

"Do you believe it?" she asked Flavius.

"I believe it!" Flavius answered firmly. "There is much I don't yet understand, but I will not rest until I know the meaning of it all, and my place in it."

"Do you believe, Alexander?" Ruth asked her oldest son.

"I do," he said without hesitation. "I know He lives."

"Do you believe, Rufus?" Ruth asked.

"Yes," was his immediate answer. "I don't understand a lot of things, but I believe that Jesus is the Son of God and that He died and has come back alive."

"Simon, my husband, do you believe?"

"I know it is true," he smiled. "I don't need to see Him, I feel it here," he said, touching his heart. "He lives!"

"He lives!" Ruth shouted, as though telling the world.